D1362076

Cinderstella

A Tale of Planets Not Princes

by Brenda S. Miles, PhD
and Susan D. Sweet, PhD

illustrated by
Valeria Docampo

MAGINATION PRESS • WASHINGTON, DC
American Psychological Association

For Vanessa, who soars with science —*BSM*

For Lauren, who has other plans —*SDS*

Published by
MAGINATION PRESS®
An Educational Publishing Foundation Book
American Psychological Association
750 First Street NE
Washington, DC 20002

Magination Press is a registered trademark of the American Psychological Association.

For more information about our books, including a complete catalog, please write to us, call 1-800-374-2721, or visit our website at www.apa.org/pubs/magination.

Book design by Susan White
Printed by Phoenix Color Corporation, Hagerstown, MD

Library of Congress Cataloging-in-Publication Data
Names: Miles, Brenda, author. | Sweet, Susan D., author. |
Docampo, Valeria, 1976—, illustrator.
Title: Cinderstella : a tale of planets not princes / by Brenda S. Miles, PhD and Susan D. Sweet, PhD ; illustrations by Valeria Docampo.
Description: Washington, DC : Magination Press, [2016] | "American Psychological Association." | Summary: In this retelling of Cinderella, Stella would rather be an astronaut and go to space than meet a prince and become a princess.
Identifiers: LCCN 2016005474| ISBN 9781433822704 (hardcover) | ISBN 1433822709 (hardcover)
Subjects: | CYAC: Science—Fiction. | Self-confidence—Fiction. | Stepfamilies—Fiction. | Fairies—Fiction.
Classification: LCC PZ7.M5942 Ci 2017 | DDC [E]—dc23 LC record available at https://lccn.loc.gov/2016005474

Manufactured in the United States of America
10 9 8 7 6 5 4 3 2 1

Once upon a time
there lived a girl named Cinderstella.

She had two stepsisters who made
her work every day. But every night,
Cinderstella climbed to her treehouse
to be close to the stars.

One day a royal invitation arrived.

"We're invited to a fancy ball!"
shrieked one stepsister.

"The prince will be there!" squealed the other.

"Princes and parties are fine,"
said Cinderstella, "but I have other plans."

"Make us dresses!" the stepsisters insisted. So that day, Cinderstella bought boxes of fabric and plenty of patterns.

But that night, she gazed at patterns,
filled with possibilities, far, far away.

"Work faster!" the stepsisters insisted the next day. So Cinderstella cut, pinned, and sewed till her fingers were sore.

But that night, she turned scraps into maps of places and planets more magnificent than she could imagine.

"Style our hair!" the stepsisters insisted the day after that.
So Cinderstella worked and weaved and piled hair high.

But that night, she reached even higher,
decorating with dreams she knew she would follow.

"Shine our jewelry!" the stepsisters insisted the day of the ball. So Cinderstella polished pearls and made sapphires sparkle.

"Don't you just love rings and twinkling things?"
asked the stepsisters.

"I certainly do," said Cinderstella, and that night she marveled at millions of rings and twinkling things. But one star shone brighter than the rest.

Cinderstella made a wish.
A wish she was working to make real.

Bäh-ling!

"Cinder, honey, have no fear. Your fairy godmother is finally here! You want to meet the prince tonight, so here's a gown that fits just right!"

"But I don't want a ball gown," said Cinderstella.

"Glass slippers, then, for your feet, and the handsome prince you soon shall meet!"

"But I don't want glass slippers."

"A golden carriage will take you there. You and the prince shall be a pair!"

"But I don't want a carriage."

"Listen, honey, you need to meet the prince so you can live happily ever after," insisted the fairy godmother.

"Why isn't anyone listening?" asked Cinderstella. "Princes. Are. Fine! But I have other plans!"

"Ah," said the fairy godmother, gazing at ribbons and stars. "Now I see your dreams— and one of them is stuck in my hair!"

She waved her wand. "A future princess you are not. Your heart has chosen astronaut!"

Bah-ling!

"Finally! My own happily ever after!"

"You earned it, Cinder, with all your stars and studying."

"Cinderstella!" the stepsisters screeched. "What on earth are you doing?"

"I'm going somewhere, too."

"Really?" they asked.

"There won't be princes, but there will be lots of rings and twinkling things. You can come, if you wish."

The stepsisters weren't certain. But they were curious.

"Let me guess," said the fairy godmother. "Parties and princes are fine, but you might have other plans, too?"

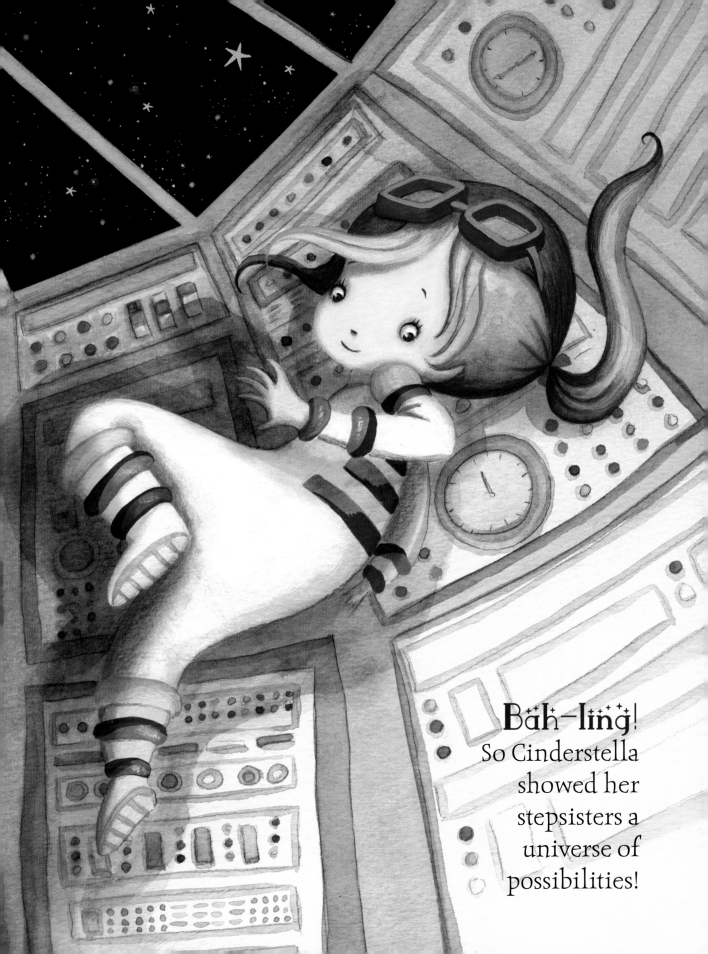

Bāh-ling!
So Cinderstella
showed her
stepsisters a
universe of
possibilities!

Sky is the Limit for Science Sisters!

Prince Finds True Love in Computer Class!

And they all discovered their own
happily ever afters.

Note to Readers

As parents, caregivers, and educators, we want every door to be open to our children, and every opportunity to be ready and waiting. We chauffeur them from lesson to lesson. We spend countless hours playing coach, educator, and mentor. And we dream about the person they will become. We do it all hoping that our children will have choices, and, most importantly, that they will be happy.

But sometimes, some doors are more open than others. While women have made huge advances in fields like law and medicine, there are still some areas where women lag behind. These areas tend to include professions collectively known as STEM.

STEM stands for Science, Technology, Engineering, and Math. While more women now attend college and university than men (and more women graduate, too), women still tend to be under-represented in these fields. So what is the challenge? Rest assured, girls don't lack the required skills and abilities to be successful in these areas. But for some reason, girls do sometimes choose other options.

Several reasons have been suggested to explain this finding. For example, girls often lack female role models in STEM. After all, when was the last time you saw a cool female physicist or mathematician in a movie or videogame? It's probably been a while. More often than not, the examples are male, and they're usually not all that flattering. Sometimes girls also lack the encouragement to pursue these male-dominated fields, or they fall victim to lingering gender stereotypes and biases about what boys and girls can and should do.

Whatever the reason, our girls may be missing out on some great opportunities. And some of our boys may be missing out, too. STEM-related jobs are on the rise, and they tend to be relatively high-status positions that often pay well. In fact, women who pursue STEM careers tend to earn higher salaries than those who work in other areas! And let's not forget that these important fields are a key part of our economy, and they need and benefit from the voices and contributions of both men and women.

Differences in STEM-related attitudes and interests tend to begin during the middle school years, so childhood is a great time to help encourage a range of possibilities! Here are a few suggestions to try:

Foster interest. Encourage your child in all subject areas, including science. You can start by making science relevant and fun. It's not as hard as you may think! Most children are full of natural curiosity. Just think about the number of questions they ask! Try directing some of those questions toward science, technology, and math. Have your child ask his or her own "why" questions, and then work together to answer them. There are many great books out there that offer scientific and technical information in engaging, kid-friendly ways. Or you can ask the questions! Ask your child what he or she finds interesting or wants to know more about. Look for opportunities to bring science into everyday life. Watch a spider spin a web, compare different types of rocks at the park, or blow bubbles and talk about why they pop. Count tree rings, discuss how rainbows appear, or guess how long it will take a snowball to melt and then time the process to find out.

Offer exposure. We all get better at things we practice. The same is true for science and math! Providing practice and exposure to science is also a great way to build your child's confidence in his or her skills. Most children will play happily with chemistry sets and microscopes. Playing games with numbers can also improve math skills. Visit your local science center, or take a trip to the library to look for books about science and technology. Who knows? You just might learn something along the way, too!

Provide encouragement. Encourage your child to be open to many areas, and to try lots of different things. Let your child know that learning something new is usually tricky at first, and that mistakes are to be expected. They are part of the learning process and have a lot to teach us! It can take time to learn new skills, too, so encourage your child to keep trying, even when challenges arise.

Dream big. Talk to your child about the many kinds of jobs people have, including those related to science, technology, engineering, and math. Help your child dream big! Has he or she ever wanted to go to outer space or build the world's tallest tower? Discuss exciting possibilities that lay beyond careers traditionally associated with either women or men.

Identify role models. Help your child discover a wide variety of role models he or she can look up to, including both men and women! In particular, women in non-traditional roles can help girls see their dreams as possible and achievable, and serve as a source of inspiration.

Watch stereotypes and biases. Deliver positive messages about the skills of both girls and boys, and avoid using language that suggests some careers are more suited to boys than girls, and vice versa. Such messages can affect a child's interest and motivation to try. Strive to provide a balanced approach when it comes to toys and activities. While it's fine for girls to enjoy dolls and ballerinas, if princess costumes are the only choice in the dress-up trunk, then being a princess becomes the only option for make-believe! Why not add an astronaut costume, too? And while it's okay to compliment girls on what they look like or wear, try to give positive reinforcement for what they think just as often.

Reflect. Take a moment to think about how you feel about math and science. Were they your favorite subjects at school? Or did you shudder when the math textbook appeared? Even if science and math were difficult for you, try to convey a positive attitude about these subjects to your child. And if your child has challenges, try to find ways to support your child's learning, rather than accepting "I give up."

With a little help and encouragement—and a lot of fun along the way—you can help spark your child's interest and keep the doors to a wonderful future wide open!

As always, for more advice or suggestions, or if you have any concerns about your child's health or development, seek the support of a licensed professional such as a pediatrician or psychologist.

About the Authors

Brenda S. Miles, PhD, is a pediatric neuropsychologist who has worked in hospital, rehabilitation, and school settings. She is an author and co-author of several books for children, including *Move Your Mood!* and *Stickley Sticks to It!: A Frog's Guide to Getting Things Done*. Brenda encourages children of all ages to dream big, find joy, and embrace adventure.

Susan D. Sweet, PhD, is a clinical child psychologist and mother of two. She has worked in hospital, school, and community-based settings and is passionate about children's mental health and well-being. Susan hopes all children follow their dreams and find their own happily ever afters.

Susan and Brenda have also co-authored *Princess Penelopea Hates Peas: A Tale of Picky Eating and Avoiding Catastropeas* and *King Calm: Mindful Gorilla in the City*.

About the Illustrator

Valeria Docampo's inspiration for her art is rooted in everyday life: the eyes of a dog, the shape of a tree, the sound of rainfall, and the aromas of breakfast. Born in Buenos Aires, Argentina, she studied fine arts and graphic design at the University of Buenos Aires. She has illustrated several books for children, notably *Tout au Bord*, *La Vallée des Moulins*, *Phileas's Fortune*, and *Not Every Princess*.

About Magination Press

Magination Press is an imprint of the American Psychological Association, the largest scientific and professional organization representing psychologists in the United States and the largest association of psychologists worldwide.